With Glowing Hearts

Reggi Allder

Dedication

To all who serve overseas, those who help at home, and those who stand and wait.

To Lee Lee for always being there.

Copyright © 2017 Updated 2023 and 2026 Reggi Allder

All rights reserved. Except for use in a review, this book may not be reproduced or utilized in whole or in part in any form by any electronic, mechanical or other means, known today or invented hereafter, xerography, photocopying or any information storage or retrieval system and is forbidden without written permission.

This is a work of fiction. Names, characters, places and incidents are the product of the author's imagination or are used fictitiously and any resemblance to actual persons, living or dead, business establishments, events is entirely coincidental.
Published by Cressmead Publishing.

ISBN 9781775128779

Books by Reggi Allder

Suspense:
Dangerous Web
Dangerous Denial
Dangerous Money
Dangerous Moves
Shattered Rules

Contemporary:
Sierra Creek Series:
Her Country Heart
His Country Heart
Our Country Heart
My Country Heart

Coming Next:
Dangerous Sisters
Growing Up in a Small Town

Chapter One

The North Atlantic 1946

Harriet Davis gripped the ship's railing as the vessel reared in the strong wind of the North Atlantic. She gasped as her only wool hat was whisked from her head to fly in the air. She might have enjoyed watching the twists, turns, and somersaults it made if it wasn't heading to the waves below.

She shivered and caught her tangled hair trying to keep it out of her eyes and looked out to the horizon to prevent the seasickness that threatened to swamp her. What had become of her good sense? She was leaving her friends and family to journey thousands of miles over the water, alone, to be with a man she barely knew?

Hoping to find protection from the wind, she slid to a sitting position. The thought of going back into the dining room, with the odor of food permeating the place, made her gag. Better to endure the cold until the luncheon meal was complete. Maybe when the weather improved, the sea would calm. Possibly, she'd manage a cracker and a bit of soup at supper time.

She recalled Mother encouraging her to leave the small Welsh village where she lived and to travel to London. Harriet, the oldest of twelve children including three sets of twins, was her mother's helper. Even so,

Mum understood her desire. They had secretly applied for admittance in a London nursing school program.

"I don't want you to stay here. You're strong and free. Go now, before the opportunity disappears. I'll miss you, but you can enjoy the life I dreamed of, but never experienced," her mother said. "Send me letters of your adventures. Leave before your father returns and sets his foot down and prevents you."

Her mum had placed one of the twins on a blanket near the sofa and sat with a sigh, opened her blouse, and put the other babe to breast. "I love my man and my babies. I willingly gave up my chance to travel in order to be with your father." The baby whined and, with the wisdom of experience, her mother had adjusted the latch on her left tit and helped the little one suckle. "Of course, I didn't think your father would be gone much of the year to make a living for his brood. Still, I've made my bed."

A week later, in the pouring rain, Harriet had taken the bus to London.

Now, three years later, instead of returning to work in her small village as planned, she was leaving the country, maybe forever. A chill ran through her. Was it the wind or the realization she'd left everything she understood?

"Harriet, you will catch your death in this wind. Come inside."

She looked up to see Tillie, her new friend, standing in the doorway holding on with one hand and beckoning with the other. "Please."

In the Mess, they sat at the table. The area was not only used for eating their meals but for a place to socialize and read. The children played in the room as well.

"Didn't the wives do a good job dressing up the place?" her friend asked. "I think it was good of the captain to allow us to decorate the walls, makes the room more like home."

Harriet nodded in agreement, though the large beige room with many tables and chairs would never pass as anyone's house. Still, the women had volunteered to put up colorful quilts and shawls on the walls to warm the austere room. The crew might find their dining room a bit changed, but she had to admit it helped the atmosphere.

"There's a surprise for you. Cook made broth for you. He found crackers too. Try and take a sip." Her friend touched her protruding stomach and then joined her at the metal table. "I understand nausea can put you off food, but…"

"That's very kind of him." She glanced at Tillie. "How is the baby?"

"Growing beautifully, thank you for asking." The woman rubbed her stomach. "I remember the nausea. I could hardly hold anything down. Are you sure you're not with a child?"

"I don't think so, only seasickness."

"Well," she shrugged, "go on and try the soup." Tillie handed her a spoon. "I liked it and I ate a bowl of it before I came to get you."

All the women had been kind, but she and Tillie had become close in the days since the ship left Britain for Halifax, Canada. Many of the wives had babies in their care. A few of them had toddlers to supervise. One mother had a two-year-old and another baby on the way.

Hattie managed to eat half of the consommé and munched a cracker. “I do feel better. Nice of you to think of me.”

“We wives must stick together.” Tillie hesitated. “You and your husband married a short time ago?”

Harriet nodded, her mouth full of soup.

“What a brave thing to do, marry someone you barely knew.”

“If you met him you’d understand.” Her cheeks burned remembering the few days she spent with her husband.

“My Harry and I have been together for three years.”

Hattie swallowed hard. “I met Alan a little more than a year ago and immediately understood he was the one for me. We only had a little time together before he was gone on assignment. We wrote to each other.”

“Oh, so romantic.” Her friend sighed. “One of the ladies told me the Canadian forces came into the war in 1939. She has been married for over five years.”

“Five years ago, I was only fourteen.”

Several children ran into the room and she watched a ball roll across the floor. A three-year-old ran after it.

Harriet picked up the ball and rolled it gently toward the young girl.

“I’m glad you did that. I don’t believe I can bend down anymore. Junior is getting so big.” Tillie laughed. “Do you want more crackers? Cook might be willing to let us.” She started to leave.

“No. Thank you. This is enough. I’m glad to eat something I can keep down.”

"Tell me about Alan Barlow. How did you meet him?"

The sound of her new surname surprised her. She still thought of herself as Miss Davis. *Mrs. Alan Barlow.* She mulled the sound of it in her mind.

"The first time I set eyes on him he was lost in London. Well, what I mean is he was looking for the hospital, but he was blocks way, having taken a wrong turn." She paused, remembering. "Later, I learned he piloted a de Havilland DH 98 Mosquito bomber. He flew over the channel to drop ordinances, do reconnaissance, and night raids. Being from a rural town in Canada, he'd never managed directions in a large city."

"My husband is from a small town as well. Somewhere on the prairies, I think."

"Maybe we'll be neighbors," Harriet said hopefully. "Alan's from a place called the Okanagan Valley. Isn't it a strange name?"

"Well, it is a foreign land."

They sat in silence and she contemplated on the gravity of her decision to marry and move to an unknown country. Vibrant and sure of himself, an image of Alan the first time they met, flashed in her memory.

Chapter Two

London, England eleven months earlier:

Night would soon fall. Harriet rushed to get inside before blackout shades covered the windows, making the streets gloomier.

A man stood on the walkway facing her. He glanced first one way and then the other. Dressed in uniform, the polished buttons down the front of his jacket and on each pocket stayed perfectly sealed. But his mouth was slightly open as if he were talking to himself, his expression confused, eyes searching for something in the dim light.

He swept off his brimmed hat and pushed his brown hair back when he saw her. “Miss.”

She didn’t talk to strangers. But something in his demeanor caused her to ask, “Are you lost?”

He grinned. “Well, I wouldn’t say exactly that. Just can’t find my way at the moment.”

“Where are you going?”

“There’s a hospital nearby. I’m visiting a friend. Dang, if I don’t seem to be going in circles. And with the rubble and missing street signs…”

He approached her, his hat still in hand, and his blue eyes now clearly visible. “I’d appreciate any help you might give.”

She hesitated. Maybe she should walk by and ignore him.

He didn't come any closer, but appeared to be waiting for her response.

"As it happens, I work there. I'll show you." Had she gone mad? She was talking to a stranger and inviting him to follow her. Mum would never forgive her for such a breach of etiquette. Harriet shrugged. With the war raging these days, things were different. Right?

"After you." He stepped back and let her pass.

She glanced at him as he caught up with her and she realized he was tall and slim, but well built. He exuded strength and the cockiness of a self-assured man.

"My buddy had himself taken out of the war. Not by a Messerschmitt, but by a British taxi," he offered. "The darned fool ran right out in front of one." He took a quick breath. "Heard the man's in traction at the hospital. With a bum knee and a broken arm, he will most likely be sent home."

"You're a flyer? We're not supposed to talk to flyboys, especially not Americans."

"I'm from the Dominion of Canada," he said proudly. "We Canucks can be trusted to be polite to women folk. Good manners are highly valued in my part of the world."

Because of the twinkle in his eye, she didn't understand if he was teasing her or not.

"Miss, you are safe with me."

"I'm glad to hear it," she responded in her stern nursing voice. She used it when a patient had to do something unpleasant, but important to their care. At eighteen, she understood her manner didn't carry the weight of the matrons in the ward, but she did her best.

He gave her a dimpled smile. "Are on your way to work?"

"I'm going to have a bite of supper first."

"Is that your food?" He pointed to a box carried on a shoulder strap.

"That's my gas mask. This is my dinner." She patted the canvas bag she held.

"You carry a mask every day?"

"It pays to be ready in case of an attack. I must be able to help the patients."

"Brave."

Was he making fun of her? A flyer who'd probably been in dogfights against the enemy wouldn't think her courageous.

"I mean it." He seemed to understand her skepticism of his statement concerning her bravery.

"Thank you." Harriet paused. "It is only a few more blocks, but the next one is rather difficult with all the rubble. An ordnance exploded a while ago."

"You say that so calmly."

She shrugged. "Part of the times." Her voice sounded cool but, inside, her stomach turned every time she passed the ruined flats where people had died. She found herself walking faster.

They had just crossed the street when an air-raid alarm wailed.

"We better go to the underground." She glanced at him to see if he was following. "The tube is at the end of the street."

People came out of the nearby structures and followed them, moving quickly toward cover.

Just before they descended, he hesitated as if deciding to go in or not. The alarm blared again and he moved forward.

While being jostled by people carrying children, bedding and supplies, they descended the flights of stairs. In the tube, the air was dank and the lights were dim.

"There's a good spot by the wall." She took his hand and led him, reaching the empty area before anyone else. She let go of him and pulled a plaid blanket from the bag and spread it on the floor. "We'll be out of the foot traffic, less likely to be stepped on. Sit down."

A surprised expression appeared on his face then instantly disappeared replaced with an indifferent one.

"Please join me—if you wish." What was she thinking telling him what to do? He wasn't her patient and he might not want to stay with her. They'd only met by accident. Used to caring for and giving orders to patients, she assumed he needed her help too. But he might dislike having a girl talking to him in a rude manner.

He sat cross-legged on the blanket and stared at her.

She blushed. "I didn't mean to be bossy." She pressed her back to the cool wall. "Mum says it comes with being a nurse."

"No problem, shows you're a natural leader. I admire a woman who can take charge." He leaned against the wall next to her. "Well equipped too, what I mean to say is with the gas mask, food, and blanket."

He looked at her and they both laughed.

"What else do you have in your magical bag?" He chuckled, a warm, deep sound that rumbled in his throat.

"Just bits and bobs." She wasn't about to tell him about the compact, brush, and lipstick.

A family holding an infant and toddler in their arms nodded and seated themselves nearby.

The tube was becoming crowded and the noise level increased. Somewhere, a baby cried and a child whined about leaving his dinner on the kitchen table.

Music from a harmonica blended with the other sounds and the aroma of cooked cabbage and the smell of stale air mingled.

On a serviette, Harriet put out sliced rye bread and chunks of cheddar cheese and set a thermos flask down. "Eat with me. I always bring extra to share. Tea?" She poured it into a cup taken from the top of the flask and handed it to him.

"What about you, Miss?"

"I'll drink from the thermos." She took a sip. "Since there are no friends or family to introduce us, may I say my name is Harriet Marion Davis?"

"I am pleased to meet you, Miss Davis. I am Royal Canadian Air Force pilot Alan Kenneth Barlow."

"Happy to make your acquaintance, Mr. Barlow."

He sat up. His eyes darted from place to place, his foot tapping out an unknown rhythm. Restless, she recognized this behavior in men of action forced to be out of the fight through no fault of their own.

"I'd like to be in the battle." He glanced toward the ceiling. "I didn't come to Britain to sit on my rump." He startled. "No disrespect to your company intended."

"None taken."

"My plane is out of commission for a few days. So, I'm grounded. That's why I got time to visit my friend."

"We can leave when the all clear sounds, but that could be hours."

He leaned back again. "Not good below ground. Prefer to be in the open."

"Tell me about Canada." She hoped to distract him. "I'm told it is big."

"You have no idea." A gleam showed in his blue eyes, the color of a sunny sky. "Big doesn't begin to describe it. When I was a kid, my father piled us into our old car and we drove from the western sea, to the mountain, prairies, to out east. It took weeks. Papa was in no hurry. I think he wanted to view our Dominion more than we did. My twin brother and I were most excited about camping all the way."

"Was your mum with you?"

"She was pregnant with my little sister at the time. But she never complained, and she was the best darned cook in the campgrounds."

"You don't say. An amazing woman."

"She is. If you met her, I think you would like my mother."

What an odd thing to say. They weren't going to even be in the same country. "I'm sure I would." She smiled. "You have a twin brother. There are twins in our family too."

"Yes, Albert. I am without a nickname otherwise we would both be Al."

She laughed. "Alan and Albert. I can see Al might be confusing at the supper table."

He grinned and put his hands behind his head and crossed his legs at the ankles. "My mother is a teacher and so is my father. Are you from London?"

"More cheddar?" she said nonsensically, surprised by the change of subject.

He brushed her arms as he reached for a chunk of cheese.

It sent an unexpected chill down her spine. She fiddled with her drink before she answered him. "I live in Wales. Though my mum is English, my father is from Cardiff. I came to London to study at a nursing college."

"You're not wearing a cap. I noticed all the nurses have caps on."

"It's in my bag. I will put it on at work."

"Of course."

The tube was bustling now and the noise had increased once again. He moved closer, presumably to hear her better.

"You prefer open spaces. Guess being a miner wouldn't be your cup of tea," she said.

"There is a fair bit of mining in our area. But not for me. Flying is the thing. In the west, the sky is wide open and the intense color of blue is indescribable, with clouds so big and puffy I could reach up a grab one for a pillow." He fluffed the imaginary cushion. "Rest my head, watch the birds dive then be brought back up on the wind currents." He paused as if remembering. "The air is completely clean. If you fill your lungs, you might almost fly like the bald eagle." He grinned. "Soar out over the cedar and spruce and continue above the lakes to the mountains."

"I wish I could be there."

"Maybe someday you will."

He must have noticed her astonishment because he added, “Canada needs nurses.”

They sat together in silence. The children in the tube settled down and someone sang a Scottish folk song as a lullaby.

In low voices, so as not to disturb anyone sleeping, they continued their conversation.

She often found casual discussions with men difficult, but Alan was different. His kind demeanor made him the exception. Her words flowed and he listened without judgment when she offered her stories or opinions. She shared upcoming plans and even admitted the war sometimes caused a sense of hopelessness.

Alan told her of his life in rural Canada and of the day he fell out of the tree in his front yard and broke his arm. He and his brother had a race to get to the highest branch. “I got to the top first. Then I then fell.” He laughed. “Papa made climbing trees off limits afterward.”

Not stingy with words, he continued, then ceased abruptly. “I can be boring and it’s been so long since I’ve talked freely. Stop me when I reach your limit to endure more.” He appeared serious. However, he winked and then smiled.

“Please continue.” She sipped her now cold tea and relaxed. “Hearing the whole world isn’t falling apart is reassuring.”

Chapter Three

The all clear boomed as morning dawned. What would they find on the streets of her adopted city?

After climbing the stairs, they finally peeked out of the underground. She sighed with relief. Though there was rubble in the street, the structures stood and there were no fires.

Dear God, don't let the hospital be destroyed.

Avoiding the debris strewn in their path, they rushed toward the emergency facility. The edifice had suffered hits with V1 and V2 rockets in July 1944 and February 1945. Now in early March, maybe the rockets had struck again.

"No damage," she cried as they turned a corner and saw the hospital.

She wiped a tear from her cheek. "Let's find your friend."

After he visited his buddy, Alan would go back to his life never to be seen again. A stranger, still she had connected with him and was reluctant to sever the tie. For him, the evening was only a way to pass the time in the underground. By now, the private information she shared was most likely forgotten.

In order to be the first to break away, she said goodbye after pointing him to the room where his friend waited. A look of surprise spread across his face. "Miss

Davis, thank you for your help." He hesitated. "I believe we share values in common that make it reasonable for us to meet again. I hold a three-day pass. It would be my pleasure to allow you to show me the city." He paused as another nurse walked by in the hallway. "If you have the inclination and time, of course."

Suddenly shy, Harriet looked down the hallway. "Today is my day off. I often work nights. I should have been on duty yesterday."

"Might I hope you will take me up on my suggestion?"

"Let me ask Sister. If she doesn't need my help, I would be happy to show you London."

An hour later, she took Alan to her small flat nearby, which she shared with three other nurses. In the lounge, decorated with furniture from the local charity shop, she offered him a seat in a club chair upholstered in faded chintz.

She didn't realize his size until he sat in the feminine armchair. "Maybe the sofa would suit you better." She smiled then introduced her flat mate, Peggy.

He stood to greet her and then sat on the chesterfield as suggested.

Peggy entertained him while she went to take a quick bath and change her clothes.

In the toilet, Hattie took a nearly dry slip from the clothesline over the tub and pulled it on. Then she brushed out her shoulder-length curls securing them with a white ribbon tied around her head with a bow at the top. She scooted as fast as possible to the bedroom she shared with Peggy, and drew on a white cotton blouse and navy wool skirt. Silk stockings were unavailable because of the war. She stepped into black pumps and grabbed her purse and gabardine coat.

Her flat mate met her in the hall. “He is handsome. Where did you meet him?”

Harriet told her and watched a shocked expression spread over her friend’s face. “Is he American?”

“Canadian.”

“Well, you be careful and watch your Ps and Qs. Those North Americans’ reputation is for fast moves.” She started to leave but came back. “Do you need cab fare? I will lend it to you.”

“The money is pinned to my brassiere as always.” She gave Peggy a hug. “Don’t worry. I’ll be fine.”

Nervous, she closed her eyes and took a slow breath. Would people consider this date a pick up? Should she go? Perhaps the right question might be, did she want to? Understanding she did not wish him to disappear from her life, she hurried to the lounge.

“What shall we see first?” he asked when she came into the room.

“Well, I don’t know about you, but I’m famished. You must be starving too. Why don’t I make breakfast for us before we leave? You can freshen up. I set out clean towels.”

“Sound good to me.” A smile sent the corners of his mouth tilting upward.

“Food coming up.” She pointed him toward the toilet and left for the kitchen.

Thankful she hadn’t used her ration of one egg for the week, she cracked it into a small bowl and added water and a bit of milk. She whipped the mixture until it was fluffy. With a touch of salt and pepper it would do nicely. Soon, two strips of bacon sizzled in a frying pan. She'd saved the meat from last week's provisions. Now it was available for Alan.

Though thin, he was a big man; how much would he eat? She guessed. Time to start the oats. With an apron tied to cover her best skirt, she hummed a big band favorite while she cooked. The kettle whistled and she moved it from the burner to make room for the frying pan and the scrambled egg.

She stopped. What if Alan thought she always entertained men in her flat? The idea hit her hard in the stomach. This was the first date who'd been allowed in the home let alone given a meal. Her face heated. He might have the wrong impression.

"Smells good in here," Alan said as he entered the room.

"Mr. Barlow, I want you to understand I don't bring men into my house. You are the first to cross the threshold and it was just…" She paused to find the right words. "Because of exceptional circumstances. You mustn't believe a mistaken notion…" Her voice faded away as she decided how to expresses her concern.

"Miss Davis, I fully comprehend the situation and acknowledge the kindness you have afforded me." He stood facing her, his eyes intense. "The war creates many a strange occurrence and we all adjust as best we are able. I'm grateful you are willing to make an exception for me," he said formally but grinned.

"Thank you." Her shoulders relaxed as she smiled with relief. "Please take a seat." She pointed to one of the chairs next to a small wooden table.

He pulled it out and sat down. “No eggs for you?”

“I want oats. Gives me energy. Tea?” No need for him to learn of the details of the Ration Book and the choices imposed. Eating on the air force, base he most likely didn’t have to worry about such things. She was aware he lived in a rural valley in Canada, and his family had chickens and a garden filled with fruits and vegetables. That much he had told her last night. How wonderful to have all that was needed and more.

They lingered over a second cup of tea, mapping out the day. First to a museum and a park before going off to shops where he might find souvenirs for his family.

“You’re not married?” she blurted out and then covered her mouth with her hand.

“Never had the time.” He chuckled. “No girl left back home either. What about you, if I may ask?”

“Nursing school and work takes up most of my time.”

“Okay. I’d like to visit the Victoria and Albert Gallery. If you don’t mind.”

“Do you paint?”

“I dabble in watercolour, but not since the war started.” His look of regret passed swiftly. “Wanted to visit the V and A exhibition to look at the Tuner and Constable landscapes. The skies remind me of home. I always told myself someday….” He hesitated. “There may not be another chance.”

The harsh words hung in the little kitchen, as gray clouds on an otherwise fine day. She shivered at the thought his death in the war might not allow him another opportunity and resisted the need to hold him to her.

"I don't know a lot about art. Most of my time was spent reading medical books. Still, I'd be happy to go with you." She'd buy him a small pad of paper and a pencil so he could draw what he saw and record his exploits to take home with him when he returned to Canada—if he survived. The thought struck a nerve and she gasped.

"Are you all right?"

"Just a spot of tea down the wrong pipe," she fibbed. To show she was, indeed, fine she swallowed another bit of liquid.

"The capital of British Columbia is Victoria. So, I have an affinity for the queen." He paused. "For lunch, I thought we'd buy fish and chips. Eat out of doors, maybe a park?"

"Hmm, nice weather. Afterward we might shop for your family's gifts."

"Perfect. By the way, my buddy is going to recover, but he obviously can't use his tickets for tonight. He gave them to me. A couple of seats for a comedy at the Stoll Theatre. What do you think?"

"Lovely."

To keep Peggy happy, she rinsed the dishes before they left.

The weather cooperated and instead of the usual rain, the sun came out mid-morning. She unbuttoned her coat and gazed up at the sky. Alan was smiling when she glanced at him.

"You're beautiful. I didn't realize last night in the dim light."

"You are too," she said stupidly and then wished she could retract it.

Chapter Four

March 1945 Okanagan Valley, British Columbia, Canada

The apple trees, planted on the forty-acre spread, bloomed early this year. There might be fruit to pick sooner than planned. Pleased, Mary Barlow smiled as she walked down the dirt road, from the white two-story farmhouse, heading toward the rural mailbox.

Every day she prayed there'd be communication from one or both of her boys. The twins had been gone for some time now. Nonetheless, she didn't miss them any less than the day they moved out.

Though he would soon deploy overseas, Albert was in a boot camp in Canada. But Alan had joined up three years ago and was stationed in the United Kingdom. A flyer with the Royal Canadian Air Force, he made her proud. But if she admitted it, her heart longed to have him at home. Willard, her husband, said to hush and keep her thoughts to herself. Their sons were doing their patriotic duty.

If Will had his way, he'd be with them. But at forty-three years of age, his expertise in farming was needed as much as fighting in one of the services. Last fall, Will and the men of the Okanagan harvested the apples and sent them to Britain after hearing fruit continued to be in short supply as most of it needed to be imported. He enjoyed sharing his tasty crop.

Of course, he had grumbled when it was suggested he was too old to fight, but she'd sighed with relief. Still, being without her older children hurt. At least her ten-year-old daughter was safe and in school. Nancy might not recognize her brothers when they returned after the war. *If they do come home.* Mary stopped that thought.

At the end of the road, she found the morning newspaper in the holder under the mailbox and tucked it under her arm. With a quick yank, she opened the metal box and claimed a utility bill. Hopeful, she peeked into the back of the box and discovered a letter. How long had it been there? She rushed to find out which son had written. To her surprise the name was from a woman she didn't know. The return address in Great Britain, the message was addressed to her husband. Curiosity burned in her. Even so, Mary didn't dare open his correspondence.

Back in the farmhouse, she tossed the envelope on the kitchen counter. It could wait until after dinner. Will had driven to the local secondary school as usual, teaching English until the late afternoon. He and young male volunteers from the school would be in the fields mulching the trees until darned near suppertime.

The knitting basket, where had she put it? As leader of the Women's Knitting Society, tardiness wouldn't be understood. The wicker sewing box sat next to the console radio. She remembered falling asleep listening to a show last night.

She and the other women knitted mittens and socks for the Royal Canadian Navy. They made a few for her boys too and she hoped they would arrive wherever Alan and Albert were stationed.

In the bedroom, she changed her clothes, pulling on a beige dress with padded shoulders. Then she stepped into brown leather Oxfords. With a rat placed on the top of her head, she covered it with her hair and held it in place with dark bobby pins. Just the style the actress wore in the last movie she and Will had attended. Satisfied a gust of wind wouldn't disturb the design, she applied red lipstick, smoothing it with her little finger and wiping her hand with a tissue. Ready to go. Her arms would ache by the end of the afternoon, but she'd be contributing to the war effort. She smiled.

After dinner, she and her daughter washed the dishes and made lunch for the morning. Later, while Nancy read her school books, she glanced at the newspaper checking the obituaries for any familiar names, thankful her sons were not among them. When their daughter was in bed, Mary retrieved the letter.

"Will, this came in the post today. Addressed to you."

"From the boys?"

"No. Never heard the name. Maybe you'll recognize it."

"I don't recall." He turned it over and checked the back of the envelope. "Nope."

"You going to read it?"

"What's your hurry? Probably a mistake. Our neighbor, Mr. McLaren writes to family in the UK. Maybe it should have gone to him."

"Honey, your name is on the envelope."

"Well, then."

He got up from the table where he was having his tea and went to a jacket hanging on a hook on the back of the kitchen door and pulled his reading glasses from the pocket.

She wanted to tell him to hurry, but didn't. He wouldn't understand she'd struggled to wait through the day to discover the secret in the post.

"Well, I'll be, can't imagine how they got my name."

He read out loud.

"Dear Mr. Barlow.

I am a teacher in the UK. My class wanted me to inform you that we received apples from you and the people of the Okanagan. Thank you. We hadn't seen apples since the war started. You can imagine the delight the children felt when they understood each would take two home with them.

Many other schools received your fruit as well. I have been asked to tell you how much it means, knowing someone thousands of miles away cared enough to share their bounty with strangers. Please tell everyone involved how thankful we were to receive your generous gift. We will keep you in our prayers.

Most sincerely,
Mrs. Randall"

"I'll be…" He took off his glasses and rubbed his eyes. "Kind of her to send this note."

He sat silent for a moment. "Where do think our boys are now?"

"Don't know." Mary hesitated. "I just pray they're safe."

***

In London, the bus was due to arrive any moment. While she and Alan waited, Harriet enjoyed the fresh air after a night in the underground. Arriving on schedule, the bus was almost full. Even so, they found seats together.

Conversation came easily and she began to think of him as a friend, though they had only known each other for a short time.

At the Victoria and Albert Museum, they walked by the sandbags stacked to protect the building from further damage as it had been bombed earlier. The hours passed rapidly while they toured the exhibitions. Art never interested her much. Still, hearing Alan's stories about Canada's always changing sky and the wide-open panoramas helped her enjoy the watercolors through his eyes. Alan's love for country was contagious and she wondered if she might enjoy visiting someday.

Over fish and chips, eaten while sitting on a park bench, she shared her tales of living with eleven brothers and sisters in a small cottage. They laughed over the antics of her little brother who had a knack for finding mud and bringing it into the home.

"Canada has no shortage of mud." He laughed. "We might be the capital of the stuff."

She giggled and again mentioned her dream of owning a large house where everyone had their own room. Perhaps she'd have a dog too someday, a Border Collie. She'd never voiced her daydreams to anyone, not even her mum. What was it about Alan that caused her to open her heart to him?

Later that evening when they left the theatre, the night turned cold and fog filled the streets. A good sign as the Luftwaffe didn't fly in heavy fog; the night would be free of air raids. "I never used to like the mist that often covers London. Not until I learned the bombers don't go up in pea soup." She buttoned her coat and unfolded a pink flowered scarf from her pocket. A Christmas present from her parents, she placed it on her head and tied a knot under her chin.

"Thank your friend for the tickets. I can't remember when I've laughed so hard." She slid her arm into the crook of his elbow.

"I can't recall being in nicer company." He patted her hand. "Where to now?"

Pleased he didn't want to leave her yet, she said, "If we hurry we can reach my neighborhood pub before last orders."

They ran to the bus stop just in time to jump on the vehicle before it left.

Laughing, she took a seat by the window and he joined her. "Luck is with us tonight."

An odd expression crossed his face. He held her hand and an electrical charge shot through her. "You might be my lucky star, Harriet."

She smiled weakly unsure what he meant. He let go of her and she shivered without his warmth.

The pub, with light wooden walls and patterned carpet, was open and a few locals populated the place. The smell of beer and chips filled the room and so did the sounds of muffled conversations. Two older men played darts, laughing and debating who won the last go around. A middle-aged couple, dressed in their best finery, sat eating at a table by the blackout draped window.

She and Alan found seats at the corner table. "Beer?" he asked.

She didn't usually drink. However, she agreed. He returned carrying two pints and she took a sip. "Hmm." She wiped her lips with her tongue. "I don't remember it tasting so good." *Must be the company.* "I'm sorry we ran out time today before we shopped for gifts for your family."

"We could do it tomorrow and there's a dance hall at the Flyer's Club too. Do you like dancing? They have a swing band and a singer."

"Sounds like fun. I haven't been to one since I started nursing school."

"Okay, good."

She took a gulp of beer. Could she coax Peggy into taking her shift at work? They often traded days off, but this was short notice.

Alan slid closer and put his arms around her shoulders. "When I came to town, I planned on seeing my buddy and then maybe going for a little R&R at the canteen and back to the base as I didn't know anyone else."

"R&R?"

"It's a Yank term, means rest and relaxation. Fun if you have someone to do it with. I thought my buddy and I were going to take it easy and then see the town." He took a gulp of beer and swallowed. "I'm sorry for his accident, but if he'd watched where he was going that night, I'd never have met you. His bad luck. My good luck." He shrugged "Fate is an odd phenomenon."

"You're quiet the philosopher, aren't you, Alan?"

"I can't deny it, but a handsome sort wouldn't you say?" He grinned.

"Get you." She laughed and leaned closer to him.

"Better drink up. We close in five minutes." The bartender shouted louder than necessary.

With reluctance, she moved away from Alan.

Outside of the pub, the fog lingered, making eerie shadows. Yet her mood couldn't be dampened. She hummed and danced to an imaginary swing tune. A bemused expression spread across his face. She was having fun, but probably making a fool of herself.

He'd been right about one thing. Fate was a wonder. She met him and now they were going to the dance hall and she felt lighthearted for the first time since coming to London. She held her arms out to him and he filled them. They waltzed down the street together. Moving as if he knew the song she had in her mind, he kept perfect rhythm to the beat.

Her head spun when they reach the flat. "I'm not used to beer," she said, suddenly nervous.

"Don't worry. You're charming when you're a bit tipsy."

"Is that what I am?" She held her fingertips to her mouth and then touched his lips with them. "Night, see you tomorrow."

She shut the door before he could kiss her, no matter how much she wanted him to. It was the first date after all.

Chapter Five

Harriet shook her friend. "Peggy, wake up!"

"What is it?" The woman sat upright in bed. "Are we going to be bombed?"

"No. Everything is all right. More that okay. It's wonderful."

"Why did you wake me in the middle of the night to tell me this?" Her friend yawned and stretched. "What time is it?"

"I don't know, but I need a favor." She sat on the edge of the bed and pulled off her shoes. She sighed.

"Can't it wait until morning?"

"No. I'm sorry."

"All right, what's the problem?" Peggy yawned again. "You might as well turn on a lamp if we are going to talk. The blackout drapes are already pulled." She propped her pillow and leaned back as if she thought it might be a long discussion.

Harriet turned on a bedside light, removed her coat and sat on her own bed facing her friend. How could she tell her story in a way that would encourage Peggy to give up her days off? "You're my best friend. I wouldn't ask you if there was another choice." She hesitated. "I'm falling for Alan." She held up her hand before her friend contradicted her. "Don't you believe in love at first sight?"

"Harriet, I'm too old and practical. I'm twenty-one and have been around the block a few times."

"Well, I believe it. In these scary days, we take love where we can."

"Harriet! You haven't done anything foolish?"

"No. I didn't even kiss him." She touched her lips remembering how much she wanted to. "He has a pass for two more days and he's asked me out. Tomorrow I'm scheduled to work the day shift." She hesitated and paced the small bedroom.

"Well, Harriet, what do you want?"

"I need you to work for me for a couple of days."

"But I have two days in a row off. How often does that happen?"

"Not frequently. I apologize, but Alan's a flyer. He might be shot down or be transferred and I'd never see him again. I'll pay you back."

"This isn't like you. You never date."

"You're right. I didn't want to get involved especially with the North Americans. I don't grasp why, but he's different."

"And you wouldn't be happy with one day?"

Harriet hung her head and waited.

"All right, but you owe me." Peggy groaned.

"Thank you. I'll never forget this. I'll give you a week, a month, whatever you want."

"Don't overpromise. I might take you up on it." She laughed. "Now turn off the light and go to bed. I have to work tomorrow."

She hugged Peggy and turned off the light.

***

The next day Hattie and Alan searched the shops. They found flowered scarves for his mother and sister and a plaid scarf for his father. "Nice and easy to ship," Alan proclaimed.

She found a pocket-sized note pad with a pencil held in a cloth bag. "You can carry it with you and draw if there's time."

"Thanks. I'll give you my first sketch."

Alan paused for a moment. "I bought something for you too. Silver bangles for your ears."

"They're beautiful, but I can't take them. We just met." She handed them back to him and hoped he wouldn't be angry.

"I will keep them until we know each other better."

The day rushed by. What was the saying about time when you were having fun?

It rained and they ran into a little tearoom for biscuits and tea. From the window, she watched people passing and guessed their names. She laughed easily. Their chats were without the usual dead spots where she begged her mind to come up with a topic and wished she'd stayed at home.

They took in a matinee movie of *The Canterville Ghost*, a comedy with Charles Laughton. Then they ate the sandwiches she'd packed.

Later that night, the band was in full swing when they arrived at the dance hall. The sets were long and she and Alan were on the floor until her feet hurt. They sat through a couple of jazz numbers, but he insisted they get up for a waltz.

Fine by her, she'd been hoping for a slow song. Her mother had told her to keep a gentleman at arm's length when waltzing. By thc end of the night while they danced, she gave in to her wish to be closer and rested her head on his chest.

"Remember we have all day tomorrow. Think of what you want to do," he whispered in her ear, sending a shiver of longing through her.

"The band played, *Good Night Ladies* and the dance floor filled with patrons.

They caught the last bus of the night to her neighborhood, then walked to the front door of her flat. He kissed her. The gentle a wisp of his lips tantalized her. Before she could call his name, he covered her lips, deepening the contact.

"Hattie, I've been waiting to do that all night." He bent toward her.

"Sorry to bother you two." Peggy peeked out of the front door. "There's been an emergency at the hospital. All staff is recalled. No days off for a while, I'm afraid."

Chapter Six

Still in Alan's arms, she held on to him. "I don't want to work tomorrow. I had such brilliant plans for us."

He kissed her cheek. "I'm disappointed too. Orders are orders. That's what they say in the service. We can write. I'll send you a drawing" He stepped away. "I can't say when I'll have more time off. Things are intensifying. I'm not allowed to say more." He stared at her as if memorizing had face. "Harriet, it's been a joy meeting you."

He was gone before she could respond.

***

In the next week, the weather improved and bombing raids increased, filling the hospital with the wounded. Patients lined the hallways, laying on gurneys.

Harriet worked double shifts, snatching naps on cots in the breakroom when time allowed.

She wouldn't be able stay at home for the night. But certain Alan would write, she made the trip home to check the post every day.

Peggy had warned her not to become too involved with him. Flyboys took pleasure where they found it and flew to the next bird.

Alan is different.

She suppressed her disappointment when nothing appeared in the post. How could she be so wrong about him?

Mum had told her that after the war things might settle back to normal. There'd be time to find someone. She'd told her to take it slow and easy. "Harriet, you're young. Enjoy your freedom. Beware of making a decision too early that will lead to a life sentence with a person you don't know. You'll repent at leisure."

All the same, she wanted Alan.

Day after day no mail came from him. She began to expect nothing and yet she looked. Her cheery and bright letters to him now seemed foolish. How naive she must appear. Her face heated as embarrassment crawled up her back. She'd poured out her heart to Alan. Dear God, she was stupid.

Enough.

This was the last day she'd bother rushing home while praying for a note from a man who didn't care. Instead of being pleased with her decision, she groaned.

A few days later, exhausted, she returned to her flat. Out of her shoes, she wiggled her toes in the soft carpet under her feet, hung her coat in the closet, and looked forward to a peaceful night in her own bed. There'd be no moving from her room until the daylight hours returned. She passed the kitchen and considered eating something. Sleep trumped food and she flopped on her bed and pulled up the covers.

Her eyes closed when the air-raid warning screeched. "No. I'm not getting up. No way." A blast shook the bedroom. Too close. With eyes wide open she listened to be sure it wasn't a nightmare.

Shit.

As the air-raid sirens blared, she ran for shelter. In the underground, sitting in the same place where she and Alan had sat, memories of him taunted her. A smile, a wink, a chuckle, and the attentive way he listened to her, why hadn't she understood he was too good to be true?

***

After more than two weeks without a day off, Harriett walked home in the rain. Why bother to check the post? Another disappointment wasn't needed. Still, she reached into the box and pulled out not one but three letters.

At first, she considered it might be misplaced correspondence. Her name was emblazoned on the front of each envelope. Alan Barlow was written neatly in the corner. She screamed and held them to her heart.

"Are you all right, Miss," a passerby asked.

"Fine." She grinned. "Isn't it a beautiful day?"

"If you say so." The elderly gentleman pulled up his collar against the drizzle and hurried away.

To keep the paper dry, she rushed into the building and up the stairs before reading them.

In the faded chair Alan had sat in, she opened the first letter.

Dear Miss Davis,

I hope this letter finds you well. I was pleased to make your acquaintance. Kind of you to make the effort to welcome a stranger into your city. As promised please find a couple of my drawings made from your considerate gift.

Sincerely,

Alan K. Barlow

Two small drawings fell out of the envelope. The first of a sky with huge clouds as he'd described when he talked about Canada. Stunned, she viewed the second one. A portrait of her smiling, dressed in the outfit she'd worn the night they'd gone out together.

The second letter was a short note. He flew more often as the number of sorties had increased and he included a sketch of his plane. He must have received her letters because this one was less formal. It started "Dear Harriet" and he signed it with his first name, no surname.

The third and final message greeted her as Hattie and he signed off, "Hoping to see you again, most sincerely, Alan."

A tear slid down her cheek. Maybe he did care at least a small amount.

***

On leave, Alan arrived in London. Hard for him to believe it had been six weeks since he'd seen Harriet, but he remembered every detail of their time together. Did she?

In the early evening, he asked the taxi driver to wait while he visited the hospital to find out if she was working. Pleased to discover it was her day off, he gave the cabbie her address.

Alan paid the fare, exited the car, and tipped his hat to the local air warden.

As he walked toward the flat, the familiar drone of a Messerschmitt sent him staring skyward. The air-raid sirens squawked as a bomb hit. The concussion knocked him off his feet.

"You all right, Sir?" The warden rushed to help him.

"Yeah. Are you?"

"I'll do."

People cried as they ran from the building, some with cuts on their faces.

"Hattie!" *Dear God, I have to find her.*

The warden grabbed him. "Sir, you can't go in. It is not safe." He restrained Alan and another man came to help hold him back.

A woman staggered out of the building.

"Peggy! Where's Harriet?"

"Oh, Alan, thank goodness you're here. I didn't see. It all happened so fast," she cried. "We were both in the lounge when she decided to grab a sweater from the bedroom. I didn't see her again." She wiped blood from her forehead.

"Help her," he shouted to the warden.

"It's fine, Sir, everything is in hand," the middle-aged man said, but refused to release his grip.

An ambulance drove up and parked. Soon, a young attendant helped Peggy to his vehicle. Just then the building shook. Stones shifted and a few fell to the ground, sending billows of dust to fill the air.

"Let go of me." He tried to shake free of the men holding him. "My girlfriend is in there. Don't you understand?"

"Sir, I don't care if Mother Mary is in there. No one is entering until the engineers tell me it's safe. Them is the rules."

"Damnit, man, don't you love anyone enough to risk your life?"

"I'm sorry, son." The old man looked at his feet.

The sound of fire engines blared. From a top window flames appeared.

Alan fisted his hand, ready to strike. “Let me go.” The man released his grip a bit and Alan yanked out his hands and ran toward the flat.

“You were warned,” the guy shouted “If you die…”

He didn’t hear the rest of the sentence because he was in the structure and focused on finding Hattie. The stairs remained, but the center of the lobby had filled with debris and dust floated in the air. Light broke through a hole in the wall. A few people rushed to the front door. None of them had seen Harriet.

Stepping over the rubble, he took the stairs. On the second floor, the air was filled with smoke, making it harder to see.

A woman coughed.

“Harriet?”

“Help me,” she gasped.

He pulled the wreckage off the young female trapped by a large chunk of damaged ceiling and fragments from the floor above her. Devastated it wasn’t Harriet, however, he carried the girl down the stairs to the front door.

“Can you walk out of here?”

“I’ll manage, thank you. God, protect you.” She hobbled out of the exit.

He ran back up to the second floor and searched as the air quality worsened. On his way to the top floor, he tripped when the building shuddered. The front door to Harriet’s flat stood open and the windows were shattered, the drapes twisted in the breeze.

“Harriet, sweetheart, where are you?” He waited for a reply. “Dear God, Harriet answer me.”

Nothing.

He moved farther into the lounge. Peggy said she left the room for a sweater, but maybe Harriet had gone out without telling her friend.

"Answer me."

"Alan." Her voice was so weak he almost didn't hear her.

Throwing broken furniture out of the way, he reached the bedroom. The room shook as if an earthquake hit the area. The warden had warned him the place might collapse.

Chapter Seven

Harriett groaned. The dresser, ceiling plaster and broken wooden studs almost hid her. Eyes open, she struggled to move.

"Harriet, sweetheart."

Smoke filtered through the broken shards of the bedroom window and the building shuddered again.

"Alan, go out before it's too late," she choked out the words. "I don't want you to die too."

"Nobody is dying."

The debris-covered tallboy was surprisingly heavy. Falling on a petite girl, her arms looked pinned under the bureau. Adrenaline surged as he tossed everything away and helped her to a sitting position. "Anything broken?"

"I—I don't think so." She coughed.

"Thank God." Fearing the place might collapse, in a swift movement, he picked her up in his arms. "I've got you and I'm never letting you go."

She smiled weakly and closed her eyes.

He carried her out of the front lobby to the waiting ambulance. There were two other people in the vehicle.

"Mister, you better sit on the curb," the attendant said. "You're shaking. Are you hurt?'

"I'm fine. Take care of her."

“We’ll will. Go and sit.”

At the curb, he stared at his hands. Harriet might have died. Gone before he could explain how much he cared. His heart thundered in his chest. He’d never considered she might die. He was the one with the dangerous profession. But he could fight back. She was, as the saying went, a sitting duck. Useless anger raged in him.

He saw her on the stretcher looking delicate and pale. For the first time in a very long time, he prayed.

“You better move, Sir. That fire isn’t getting any smaller,” the warden said, pointing to dwelling he’d just exited. “I’m glad you found your lady friend.”

Alan nodded to the man. The gentleman was only trying to do his job and Alan hadn’t made it any easier for him. He moved closer to the ambulance as the doors shut. “What the…”

“It’s okay,” the warden said. “The driver tells me he is transporting both the women to the local hospital for observation. As they can’t come back here… Well, you best meet them. Do you need directions?”

“No. Uh, thank you.” He set out at a run, dodging the hoses and wreckage that littered the street.

He found Peggy in the emergency waiting room. “Are you all right?”

“I’m fine. Sit with me, Alan. The doctors are looking her over, but she will be okay too.”

“Thank God,” he whispered.

An hour later, Harriet walked into the waiting room dressed in a nurse’s uniform, a bandage on her arm and a bruise forming on her right cheek. He rushed to her. “I thought I’d lost you. You’re okay?”

“Yes.” She smiled. “I owe you my life.”

"Hattie, you are my life." He held her gently to him.

"I love you, Alan."

***

Harriet didn't know how he finagled the time off but, three weeks later, they married in her local church. She wore a white suit with a peplum and a sweet little hat with a short tulle veil. He looked smart in his dress uniform.

One of his buddies played the wedding march on his harmonica.

Her mother and father attended as did Peggy and several nurses. Alan's best friend, now out of the sickbay, and a couple of flyers from his air base stood up for him.

Peggy took photos. They held the reception in the hospital cafeteria. The kitchen staff surprised them with a small single layer cake made with donated flour and sugar rations. With red icing, they wrote "Congratulations Mr. and Mrs. Alan Barlow" on the top of the cake.

They spent a glorious honeymoon weekend in Hastings by the Sea. Then he reported back to his air field.

Chapter Eight

Halifax, Nova Scotia, Canada 1946

Eleven days after Hattie left the United Kingdom, the ship docked at Pier 21 on schedule. She said goodbye to the many friends made on board and promised to keep in contact with them. Now, all she could think about was being with Alan.

After disembarking, she stood in the annex near the pier, a temporary wooden shed built after a fire a year earlier. Impatient, she waited in the queue until, finally, her paperwork was processed.

On the way out, she noticed a man tall enough to be Alan, right colour hair, similar carriage, but something felt wrong. He looked up and smiled. Not Alan.

She stopped, blocking the doorway. Where was her husband?

"Excuse me," a woman said. "May I get by?"

Trembling and holding her suitcase and tote bag with Alan's precious drawings inside, she exited the annex.

The man she'd seen held out his hand. "Hello, I'm Albert Barlow."

She stared blankly at him. "How did you know me?"

"Alan sent a drawing of you. I'd know you anywhere."

"Where is he?"

"He's missing." Stress pulled at the corners of his mouth and his eyes narrowed. "His plane went down in bad weather."

"No! The war's over. It can't be true." She sagged and he put his arm around her.

"Please, don't cry. We have to believe they'll find him. He told me how strong and brave you are. Harriet, be strong for him now."

Unable to speak, she nodded, stood away from him and gripped the tote bag as if it were a lifeline.

He took her suitcase. "Let's pick up the rest of your luggage. I've come to take you home."

"Home?" Without her husband, she didn't have one.

The Okanagan Valley, three months later

In the aftermath of the war neither she nor the family heard from the Minister of National Defense or the Royal Canadian Air Force. Alan's family worried, but managed a better outward face than she did. "No news is good news" was her mantra. But if he was alive, why didn't he write?

At night alone in his childhood bedroom, she dreamed of Alan and let her tears to flow. Still, she managed to keep crying to a minimum in the daylight. Remembering him saying, "You're strong and brave," gave her the desire to carry on, but for how long?

The Barlows welcomed her into the family. A sign of it was the small wedding photo she gave them. It was now framed and placed on the mantel in the lounge next to other relatives' pictures.

She did her best to understand the family and to fit in to the culture, though she had the feeling she was a reminder of their loss. Why had she survived and not their son?

Alan's young sister was a joy and she spent time with the girl whenever possible. Nancy appeared to like her as well.

In the rural area, it was difficult to go into town without a vehicle. She pined for London. Even though much of the city lay in ruins, she missed walking to visit her friends. She wrote to Mum, but didn't tell her Alan was missing. Her family was so far away; no need to worry them.

The hot and dry days of summer made a blue sky the color of Alan's intense eyes. She wandered the acres that were a wedding gift to him from his parents. She wanted to keep the faith, but sometimes found it hard to believe he would return.

His mother's depression increased as time went by without word of her son. Alan had spoken vividly of the woman. Now, Mary seemed dull and more exhausted every day. She rarely left the couch and was bothered by headaches. At a loss, Hattie did what she could to help.

"Harriet, do you mind going to the mailbox today? I'm not up to it." Mary heaved a sigh.

"I'd be happy to." She slipped on loafers. It'd be a relief to leave the house. Though large, it was beginning to close in. The screen door snapped closed. She took a breath of clean air, no smell of bombs or smoke from the burning rubble. Perhaps, all this quiet and tranquility gave too much time to think. If she took a job, would that help her endure the long days without Alan?

An eagle soared in the blue, wings flapping and then gliding on the air currents. Fascinated, she stared and wished she could share it with her husband.

A decision must be made, leave Canada or stay. What would Alan want? Did it matter if he was gone? The United Kingdom was calling. With reluctance, she admitted it might be time to leave. She groaned.

Continuing down the dirt road toward the post box, she kicked a stone out of the way. It somersaulted and tumbled to the shoulder of the dusty path.

"Good kick. Have you thought of joining a soccer team?" A man chuckled.

Still in uniform, hat pushed back on his head and eyes squinting in the bright sun, Alan stood a few feet away from her.

"My God, Alan!"

She ran to him and he dropped his duffle bag, pulled her into his arms and swung her around until she was dizzy. He kissed her until she was short of breath. "Did you miss me?" He grinned.

Tears of joy streamed down her cheeks.

He laughed and brushed them away. "The days of crying are over, Hattie."

"Alan, my love, welcome home."

*****

Author's notes:

I liked the characters of Harriet and Alan so much I imagined the rest of their lives together. Harriet and Alan Barlow were married for sixty-two years. They had four children, eight grand-children and twenty great grand-children. He became a commercial pilot and they returned many times to visit her family in the UK. She had a long career as a nurse, rising to become head of nursing at a large metropolitan medical center and later taught at a university nursing school. On their land in the Okanagan Valley, they cultivated Cabernet Sauvignon grapes and made award-winning wine.

This is a work of fiction. However, according to research, after World War II approximately 47,738 war brides and 21,950 children and babies came from the United Kingdom to live in Canada. The government set up the Canadian Wives' Bureau to help them get settled. 1.1 million Canadians served in WWII, 200,000 in the Royal Canadian Air Force.

During World War II, the Okanagan Valley framers sent fresh apples to the school children of Britain.

The title of this story comes from the Canadian National Anthem.

"With glowing hearts, we see thee rise, the True North strong and free."

Many American flyers also served in WWII and were posted in the UK. About seventy thousand women came to the United States as wives to American service men.

About the author

Reggi Allder writes suspense, contemporary novels and has written a historical novella. She contributed to two cookbooks and has written children's stories. She studied creative writing and screenwriting at the University of California Los Angeles (UCLA). She enjoys hearing from her readers. If you enjoyed her books, please check out her other novels, leave a positive review, and tell your friends about her books.

Books by Reggi Allder

Suspense
Dangerous Series:
Dangerous Web
Dangerous Denial
Dangerous Money
Shattered Rules

Contemporary
Sierra Creek Series:
Her country Heart
His Country Heart
Our Country Heart
My Country Heart

Coming Next:
Dangerous Sisters
Growing up in a Small Town

www.ingramcontent.com/pod-product-compliance
Lightning Source LLC
LaVergne TN
LVHW012340100826
845148LV00018B/3220

9781775128779